Finding a Fairy

Diana Molly

Introduction

It's sunny, bright and warm. So why not to organize a wonderful dance party? The fairies of the forest decorate and get the dancing area ready with big excitement, looking forward to the pleasant evening.

It turns out that Fountain's dance moves make the others get in laughing fits, making her offended. Little did they know that Fountain would be so hurt that she would actually run away?

They set to look for her at night, when it's dangerous in the forest. Will the power of friendship help them to save her from the terrifying danger she has got into?

.

Chapter 1. Party Decorations

The afternoon sun was shining brightly, filling the surroundings with pleasant warmness and golden sunrays. The forest was fresh and green, and the happy notes of the pretty birds rang happily from the branches of the trees. The weather was promising, and it seemed to be the perfect day for organizing the long-awaited dance party that the forest fairies were looking forward to.

Camellia was in her pink flower-house, putting on her most beautiful pink dress. She straightened her dress and clicked her fingers, which created sparkling fairy dust. The sparkles landed on her dress, making it shine and glitter. Camellia smiled: she liked her dress. Then she made sure that her hair was looking good with all the beautiful flowers in it, and left her flower-house to join her friends.

The fairies were grouped in the middle of the forest, admiring their dresses and chatting happily. There were nearly all the fairies of the forest – the fairies of the grass, the trees, the mushrooms, the wind, the river, the rainbow, the clouds, the fire, the sunshine, the fountain and others. Each one of them was wearing a beautiful puffy dress in their favorite color.

"Hi everyone!" Camellia called, coming up to them. "What magnificent dresses you all have got!"

"Yours is also very beautiful, Camellia," Grassina said, smiling.

"Thank you!" Camellia said.

"I can't wait to start the party!" Shampina exclaimed.

"Now let's start decorating, so that by the evening the forest will be ready for the dance party," Camellia said joyfully.

"Oh, I love decorating!" Raya exclaimed.

"I have never decorated in my life!" Fountain said softly. "It seems so interesting to me!"

"Now you'll see what a wonderful thing it

is," Willay said.

"Everyone must participate, as it is so much fun," Shampina said. "I remember when I was decorating a dance party place when I was little; I used to collect all the colorful decorations after the party ended, so I had tons of garlands at home to play with."

"And what did you do with them afterwards?" Grassina asked, who was already very curious about the 'tons of garlands'.

"I pretended to be organizing my own dance party," Shampina said. "I started singing and dancing until it was night already and I was sleepy."

"Oh, Shampina, it sounds so much fun!" Raya exclaimed. "We can play with our garlands after the dance party, too."

"What a wonderful idea!" Fountain said, clapping her hands.

"Good afternoon! We can also help!" The two pretty butterflies – Pinky and Viol came together with their other butterfly friends. "Please give us something to do! Whatever it is, we want to do it, to help the forest fairies in their organization of dance party!"

"Can we help you?" Viol asked, whispering.

"Of course you can!" Camellia said, giggling.

Then she clicked her fingers and many beautiful and colorful flowers appeared around them. The flow of the flowers was so strong and long, that soon enough the entire ground around the fairies was covered in colorful flowers, ready to be made into garlands.

"Now we must put these flowers together onto a string and make garlands!" Camellia said, giving each fairy a long piece of thin branch. "You can put the colorful flowers onto the strings, and the garlands will be ready in no time!" She added, showing how they should do it.

All the fairies took to work immediately. The flowers were many and it would keep them busy for a long time. They sat down in a wide circle on the green grass and started making the garlands. The colorful flowers started decreasing from the ground, while the garlands were becoming longer and fuller.

"It's so interesting," Fountain exclaimed. Her eyes were shining with pride and excitement that she was preparing the dancing area for the dance party that she wanted to go so much.

When the garlands were ready, Blowie – the

fairy of wind – flew up and attached the ends of the strings onto different trees, and soon the dancing area was surrounded by colorful garlands made from real flowers.

"I think we need some puffy white clouds as chairs," Fluffy said and clicked her fingers. Immediately many white puffy clouds appeared, which she positioned around the dancing area, so that the fairies could sit on them.

"And now I think some colorful rainbows will be a nice decoration," Rainbow said, clicking her fingers. Big and small rainbows appeared in the air, covering the dancing area like a ceiling.

"And while we dance in the evening, it will be dark, so I guess we shall need some lights," Raya said, smiling. She clicked her fingers and created many sunrays, long and short, wide and narrow, and positioned them onto the ceiling made from rainbows. The dancing area started glowing with the golden sunrays.

"I think the sitting area needs to be softer," Grassina said, pointing to the puffy clouds that were situated around the dancing area. She clicked her fingers and the grass that was under the puffy clouds started to grow longer, until it looked like a lush green carpet.

"Wow, now the place looks magical!" Fountain said.

"And what do you want to do to make the place even more beautiful, Fountain?" Camellia asked her.

"I?" Fountain asked, a bit taken aback. She had no idea how she could add to the decorations. "I don't know."

"I suppose you can create a fountain by the side of the sitting area, so it will add freshness to the entire decorations," Shampina suggested and everyone agreed.

Fountain stood at the edge of the dancing area and clicked her fingers, looking excited. At once a high fountain of crystal clear water shot out from the ground. The fountain was situated in a small glass bowl, decorated with white beads.

"Oh, Fountain, it is beautiful!" The fairies exclaimed.

"Now the area is perfectly decorated," Camellia said happily, looking around and clapping her hands.

Fountain was very proud that she had participated in decorating the dancing area.

"And now what are we going to do?" She asked.

"I think we must add some fairy dust to make it look even more magical," Willay said. On the count of three, all together. One, two, three!"

All the fairies clicked their fingers and created sparkles of different colors. The sparkles filled up the air, making it glitter and shine, and they also filled the air with sweet pleasant aroma.

"I can't wait for the dance party to begin," Fountain said.

The sun was setting. It was almost evening. The surroundings were getting darker, but their dance area was shining, glittering and sparkling in all the colors of the rainbow, and the sunrays that Raya had created were lighting it brightly, as if the sun was inside the place.

"How are we going to get the music?" Fountain asked.

"The birds will help us," Willow said. "Let's call them now and the party will begin!"

"Pretty nightingales, sparrows, canaries, grosbeaks and robins, please come over here! We need you!" Camellia called, looking around at the trees.

Rustle of wings was heard, as many birds came, flying through the thick branches of the trees, that were surrounding the fairies. They flew and perched onto the lowest branches of one of the trees nearest the fairies. They were many different birds, and all of them looked beautiful.

"What do you need us for?" One nightingale asked in a pleasant voice.

"We are organizing a dance party tonight, and would like you to help us with the music," Camellia said.

"Yes," Willay added. "You sing best of all, so we decided that your melodies will be perfect for our party."

"Do you agree to sing for the party?" Grassina asked.

The birds became very happy.

"We would love to," the robin exclaimed.

"Oh, this is so exciting!" the sparrow said.

"Wonderful!" Blowie said. "That means that we can already start our party! Girls, get ready! Let the party begin!"

The fairies giggled, and the birds got ready

to sing the best songs that they ever knew.

Chapter 2. Let the Party Begin!

The fairies went and sat down onto the puffy and fluffy white clouds that were situated on the high green grass, as the birds started to sing. It was a magical melody, sometimes slow and gentle, sometimes fast and rhythmic.

"Come on, let's dance!" Camellia exclaimed and got up. She started to dance like a flower, putting her hands up gently, and then bringing them down, while softly jumping on her toes.

The other fairies joined her. They all danced very beautifully. Grassina flew up and down, clapping her hands, Willay moved her hands fast and shook her long hair, Blowie moved her hips in rhythm of the music and Shampina moved her shoulders, walking back and forth.

"Fountain, come, join us!" Shampina called.

Fountain got up happily and went to join the other fairies. She put her hands together and took them from side to side, while moving her body from left to right, like a snake. It was the only way she could dance, and unfortunately her hair stood on ends when she danced like that. Now it wasn't an exception. Her hair shot into the air and sprang into all the directions, standing stiffly like sticks.

The fairies stopped dancing and stood there, staring at her. Then they started giggling. Willay even burst out laughing.

"Fountain, why are you dancing like that?" Blowie asked through fits of laughter. "You look like a lightning fairy!"

"Or the snake fairy!" Grassina added, giggling. "The way you move from side to side!"

"You scared me with your hair, too," Fluffy said. "It looked like lightning."

"Oh, come on, Fountain, it was really funny!" Raya said. "But I still don't understand why your hairs stand out right now like they are sticks."

Her comment made the other fairies laugh hysterically. Only Camellia wasn't laughing. She was looking rather serious. She looked at Fountain, who was just standing there, her hair standing on end, and saying nothing. Fountain looked sad and it seemed like she'd cry any minute.

"Girls, please, stop talking about the way she's dancing!" Camellia said hurriedly.

"Why? Did we say something wrong? We're having fun!" Shampina said merrily.

"Besides, just look at her hair!" Rainbow added. "Doesn't it make you laugh?"

The fairies continued laughing and having a good time discussing Fountain's dancing and her hair.

Fountain turned and flew out of the dancing area, tears spilling everywhere.

"Why did you do that?!" Camellia asked her friends, who were still laughing.

"Did what?" Blowie asked, looking around.

"Why did you laugh at her?" Camellia asked. "You hurt her, and now she's probably sitting behind the tree and crying!"

"Hurt her? How?" Willay asked. "I don't think we hurt her. She shouldn't get hurt, anyways, because we didn't say anything wrong."

"Yes, you did," Camellia said. "You were

teasing her. You we kind of bullying her."

The fairies looked at one another, shrugging.

"Camellia, what's happening to you?" Rainbow asked her. "Don't you know that we're like that? We always tease one another, and none of us ever gets hurt."

"Yes, for example, do you remember when Shampina told me to go and live in the sky, because that's where clouds were?" Fluffy said. "Of course I knew she was joking, so I didn't get hurt."

"And do you remember when Grassina and Blowie had decided to lock me up in the tree when I was changing my dress there?" Willay said. "It was about a week ago. I told them to let me out, but they told me that I was like a woodpecker and should behave like one."

The fairies started laughing again at the memories.

"Girls, I perfectly know you and know that you didn't mean to hurt her," Camellia said. "I know that you were just joking. But Fountain isn't used to that kind of jokes, because it's the first day that she's with us. She can get hurt easily."

"How boring!" Raya said.

"Don't forget that she wasn't very confident when she first came here today," Camellia said. "She was afraid that you would make fun of her or the way she danced."

"Then she probably knew that she danced in a funny way," Shampina said. "What's wrong if we pointed it out?"

"You mustn't do that, Shampina," Camellia said. "You must always consider the others' feelings when speaking. And hurting others is so easy! Bringing them back is what's difficult."

"I don't think it's difficult to bring her back," Blowie said. "I'll call her back now and we shall continue dancing. We shall ask her not to get hurt by our jokes."

Before anyone could say anything, Blowie left the dance area and flew some distance.

"Fountain?!" She called. "Please come back! We want to apologize if we hurt you! Please come back so that we can continue the dance party. We don't want to continue it without you!"

The fairies listened. But there was no answer.

"Fountain, please come back," Camellia called, slowly flying around the dance area, looking behind every tree and bush. "Your dancing was beautiful, really. The girls were only joking!"

"Yes, we were," Raya, Shampina and Willay called together. But there was no response. Even the birds were silent. The fairies looked at one another, shrugging. Then came Blowie, looking a bit confused.

"Girls," she said. "I've looked nearly everywhere in the surroundings, but I didn't find her."

"What do you mean?" Camellia asked, coming forward, looking worried.

"She's gone, girls," Blowie said. "She has disappeared."

"Maybe she's hiding somewhere?" Rainbow suggested.

"I've looked nearly everywhere," Blowie said. "And I apologized, too, but she didn't even make a sound. So she's not around here, I guess."

The fairies looked at one another, hoping that one of them had the answer, but no one had.

"Girls, let's go looking for her," Camellia suggested.

"It's such a pity that our beautiful dance party got ruined," Shampina started whining. "I want to go back and dance."

"Me, too," Willay said. "Let's continue our dance party, and when she returns, she can join us."

"But what if she doesn't return?" Camellia asked.

"She will," Grassina said. "Once she hears the melodies and our happy voices, she will return."

Camellia shook her head.

"Girls, I don't think so," she said. "Everything is much more complicated. We must go and find her. We have made a mistake by hurting her, and now we must correct it."

Chapter 3. Where Are You, Fountain?

The fairies didn't want to leave the party and to go looking for Fountain, but Camellia insisted, so they agreed.

"She went this way, so let's start flying," Camellia said.

Grassina, Blowie, Willay, Shampina, Raya, Rainbow and Fluffy followed her. The others chose to stay. It was already dark, as the sun had set hours ago.

"Here," Raya said, clicking her fingers and creating several flashlights made of sunrays. "These are flashlights for us, so we can see where we're going." She gave them to each of the fairies, and they lit their ways while flying. "But please be careful with them – they can break easily."

"What beautiful flashlights," Camellia said. "Thanks a lot!"

"Thank you, Raya!" The other fairies said, taking their sunshine flashlights.

"Fountain! Please come out and join us!" Willay called. "We really want to go back to our dance party!"

"It doesn't work, Willay," Blowie said. "She can't hear us. Camellia is right – she is probably far away now."

"Do you think she got hurt too much?" Shampina asked.

"Maybe, who knows?" Blowie said.

"All right, let's go and find her, but I don't know where," Shampina said.

They had already flown a long way, when suddenly Raya's flashlight cast light onto a leaf and she gasped.

"What is it, Raya?" Camellia asked, as the fairies stopped.

"Look!" Raya said, kneeling. The fairies lit the place with their flashlights. There was a bush there, and on the bush there was a piece of light blue fabric, which looked like it had been torn.

"It's a piece of her dress!" Camellia exclaimed, picking up the fabric. "I think she sat here to take a rest or something, and her dress ripped a little while flying away from the bush. So we are going in the right direction."

The fairies nodded.

"Good," Willay said. "Now we know that we'll find her soon."

The fairies continued flying, more hopeful than before, though from time to time some of them started complaining again.

"I wish we were dancing right now," Shampina said.

"Yes, me, too," Grassina said. "When I think how we left the dancing area and the entire party was ruined, I'm getting angry at Fountain."

"How could she do that to us?" Blowie said. "Didn't she see that we were having a party?"

"We decorated the place and had just started the party," Raya said. "And she ruined everything."

"Listen, girls," Camellia said. "Why are you blaming her for ruining the dance party?"

"Who else can we blame?" Rainbow asked, looking surprised.

"Yourselves," Camellia said. "If you didn't tease her, she wouldn't get hurt. It's that simple."

"Maybe you're right, but it still doesn't make me change my mind about wanting to go back and to continue the party," Shampina said.

The other fairies nodded, except Camellia.

"Imagine if you were in her place," she said. "What would it be like, if your friends left you in possible danger and went to dance?"

"But she's not in danger," Willay said.

"Maybe she is," Camellia said. "Nobody knows where she is now, so she may be in trouble, too. If you became friends with her today, then you must be kind and nice with her."

"Yeah, kind of like, until she realizes that we can joke sometimes," Blowie said, and the fairies giggled.

The fairies were flying through the dark forest, and the more they flew, the further they got from their homes. The surroundings were becoming strange to them – probably because of the darkness, but also it was possible that they weren't familiar with these places.

"Girls, have we ever been to these places?" Camellia asked, looking around, while carefully casting light to the surroundings. She saw strangely shaped trees and heard a river flowing somewhere nearby.

"I guess not," Willay said. Grassina closely followed her.

"Me neither," Rainbow said, holding Raya's hand.

"Well, this seems like a strange place in the forest," Blowie said.

"But are you sure that we're still in the forest?" Fluffy asked. "We've been flying for hours. It's already past midnight. We could be anywhere!"

"Help!" Someone's shriek came from nearby.

The fairies looked around in alarm, casting their flashlights here and there, trying to see who was shrieking.

"Girls, where is Shampina?!" Camellia asked, noticing immediately that one of them was missing.

"Help me, girls!" The voice came again. This time the fairies recognized the voice: it was Shampina!

"Where are you Shampina?" Blowie screamed, casting light here and there but failing to find her.

"Inside the big red flower!" The answer came.

All the fairies started to look for the big red flower. It wasn't difficult to find, as the voice was coming right from the inside of it. At last Willay found the flower and flew towards it.

"I've found the flower!" She screamed breathlessly. The flower was rather big. It was nearly her height and had large petals that were closed tightly. The other fairies followed her.

"Are you inside, Shampina?" Rainbow asked, trying to touch the flower. It shook violently.

"Yes," Shampina called from inside the flower. "But you must be careful! This flower is a savage!"

At that word the fairies flew a few steps backwards.

"What do you mean?" Grassina asked.

"How can a flower be a savage?"

"It can eat you," Shampina called. "I sat onto it only for a second to catch my breath, when its petals opened up and I fell inside. Ouch!"

"What was that?!" Willay asked, looking terrified.

"It's eating me! It wants to chew my wings," Shampina's voice came. "Please, each one of you take one petal and bring it backwards, so that it won't swallow you, too, all right? Then I'll try to fly out of it."

Even though it was rather scary, the fairies did as she had asked them. Each of them stood behind one petal and got ready.

"On the count of three," Grassina said. "One, two, three!"

They carefully opened the red petals of the flower, even though it was difficult, and watched as Shampina flew out of it.

"Now all at once, please let go of the petals!" Shampina said.

They did as she said, and the petals slammed shut like sharp teeth. Finding that the supper was gone, the savage flower started to turn its head around, trying to find someone new. It writhed and shook; opening and closing its petals like a mouth and turning its head to the sides. Then it started moving towards them.

"Fly away!" Shampina shrieked. "It's coming!"

The fairies screamed and flew faster than usual.

"But how does it move when it has roots under the ground?" Fluffy asked.

"It is a magical flower," Camellia said. "There are several kinds of different magical flowers in the deepest parts of the forest that we don't know of."

Blowie looked back, casting her flashlight, and let out her breath, relieved.

"You can calm down now, girls," she said. "The flower isn't following us anymore."

"Oh, wonderful!" Grassina said. "What a scary thing it was."

All the fairies started cheering, except Shampina. She was silent and serious.

"Shampina, are you all right?" Rainbow

asked.

"Why are you so sad? Has the flower really bitten you?" Raya asked, casting her flashlight at her wings to have a closer look.

"Girls," Shampina said. "The thing is, I feel bad now, because you helped me. You didn't move on without me. You endangered yourselves to rescue me. You are good friends. A good friend will never leave her friend in trouble. Not like me… I was ready to go back and dance instead of looking for Fountain."

"Shampina, I am glad that you feel that way," Camellia said. "It means that you will change for the better."

Shampina smiled, together with her friends.

Chapter 4. Challenges for the Fairies

The fairies were flying, hoping to find Fountain soon.

"Fountain, where are you?" Camellia was calling, but there came no response.

"I really hope we'll find her tonight," Willay said, yawning. "Ouch, what was this?"

"What's happened, Willay?" Camellia asked.

"I think a scourge of mosquitoes just had supper on my face," Willay said, slapping her face with both hands angrily, trying to wipe away the mosquitoes that were biting her face nonstop.

"Oh, yes, they are kind of active at night, aren't they?" Raya asked.

"Yes, and they are all over my face!" Willay said, sounding annoyed. "They are so many! Ouch!"

"I don't like mosquitoes' bites," Grassina said. "Those bites itch really badly."

"My face has started to itch!" Willay said, sounding frustrated.

The light of Camellia's flashlight fell onto Willay's face, and the fairies gasped: it was swollen and red. She wasn't beautiful anymore. Her eyes were bulging out from her swollen and red face, which looked like a balloon.

"Why are you staring at me like that?" Willay asked, clueless of what had become of her face.

"N... nothing," Camellia murmured and put away her flashlight from Willay's face.

"Has something happened to my face?" Willay asked, touching her cheeks with her hands.

"No, everything is fine," Shampina said. "Just a little bit swollen, but that's it."

"And it's pretty normal that it's a little bit swollen," Grassina said. "Because mosquitoes have bitten you. It will go away soon."

"Girls, do I look ugly?" Willay's voice was shaking from nervousness a little.

"No, Willay," Blowie said. "You look pretty normal. And please stop talking about your face. Let's talk about something else."

But Willay was silent. She needed to make sure that she was as beautiful as before.

"I think I can see a small lake sparkling under the moonlight over there," she said. "I want to go and look at my face in the mirror of the lake."

Before any of the fairies could say anything, Willay flew off to the lake and looked into it, casting the sunshine flashlight into the lake, so that she could see better. Seeing her swollen and red face, Willay gasped: she didn't look beautiful. Willay knelt down by the lake, getting engrossed in her thoughts. She felt bad because her friends hadn't teased her for her appearance, but had told her that it was normal to have swollen face after the mosquitoes' bites. They hadn't made jokes about her face, as she could probably do to others. *'I will change for the better as well,'* she thought, then got up and flew back to her friends, who were patiently waiting for her under one of the trees.

"Thank you, girls," Willay said, looking at the astonished faces of her friends. "Thank you for not making fun of me. Now I understand how important it is to consider others' feelings before talking. I would certainly not like it if you teased me for my swollen face. I will also try to consider others' feelings when talking, from now on."

Camellia merely smiled: she was becoming happy that her friends were seeing the truth about friendship and kindness.

"The swelling will go away soon," she said. "It will be gone in no time, believe me."

Willay nodded, smiling happily, as they flew forward again together.

"Do you think there is still a lot of way to go?" Grassina asked.

"I thought we would find her sooner," Blowie said. "As fast as a click of fingers," she added, clicking her fingers to show how fast she had been hoping they would find Fountain. But when she clicked her fingers, she clicked them too hard, and immediately a horrible wind started like a hurricane.

"Oh, what is that?" the fairies got blown away backwards in different directions. Luckily they managed to hold onto the branches of the trees and remained that way until the wind stopped blowing. Blowie was trying to stop it by clicking her fingers again, but she was only making it worse: the hurricane became so strong, that the wind ripped Blowie's wings and if she hadn't caught them in time, they would be gone forever.

The wind was so strong, that the fairies couldn't hear anything else than the blowing whistles. They knew Blowie was shouting something, but they couldn't hear her. They knew Blowie had to manage it by herself, as she was the fairy of the winds, so there was no point in trying to stop Blowie's wind: they would put themselves in danger if they moved away from the trees' branches.

At last Blowie managed to stop the hurricane with much difficulty. The fairies got down the branches and flew towards Blowie. She was not in the air – she was standing on the ground, holding both of her wings and looking very sad.

"Blowie! Your wings! What has happened to them?" Camellia exclaimed, seeing that she couldn't fly anymore.

"I am so stupid," Blowie said. "I created the wind and it ripped off my wings. I didn't want to create the wind – it was an accident. Now I can't fly and will have to walk. I will make it slower for you."

"Don't worry, Blowie, we can carry you," Shampina said and all the other fairies agreed.

Blowie looked at them in disbelief.

"Are you serious, girls?" She asked. They all nodded, smiling. "Girls, now I understand what it means when someone needs help. And the most important thing is that she is surrounded by kind friends. I feel so bad for bullying Fountain now…"

Camellia smiled. One more fairy was becoming nicer and kinder. Apparently nature had its own ways of teaching things.

"Of course we shall help you, Blowie, do not worry about it," Camellia said.

As they continued flying, Shampina and Rainbow held Blowie and carried her with them.

"It's so dark, I can't see anything," Grassina said after a while.

"Well, use your sunshine flashlight then," Raya said. "It's especially for lighting our way."

"I know, but it's still dark, I can't see where I'm flying," Grassina complained.

"Oh, Grassina, please be careful," Camellia said. "There are tree branches all the way in front of

31

us. Be sure not to hit one of them."

"All right… Ouch!" Grassina screamed and slowly descended onto the ground.

"Grassina!" Willay shouted, getting down after her. The other fairies also got down, Rainbow and Shampina holding Blowie.

Camellia flew downwards, trying to see what had happened.

Grassina was sitting on the grass, holding her knee and patting it gently.

"Grassina, what happened to you?" Camellia asked her, kneeling down beside her.

"I didn't see the branch, Camellia," Grassina said softly. "I am so clumsy – right after your warning, I hit a big and hard branch, and all I can remember is my knee hurting. I guess I have broken my leg."

"Too bad, Grassina," Rainbow said. "What are we going to do now?"

"I can fly," Grassina said. "After we find Fountain and bring her back to our home forest with us, then I can heal my leg. But before it gets healed, I won't be able to dance beautifully anymore," she added sadly.

"It's all right," Camellia said. "We'll heal your leg, don't worry."

"But when I dance, it will be ugly. I feel so bad. Now I understand how unconfident Fountain had been when we were dancing," Grassina said. "And I was so insensitive to laugh at her dancing. Now I understand how wrong I've been."

"I know," Camellia said, smiling. "Nobody will laugh at you, or at any one of you, girls, and hopefully you will become nicer to the others, too."

"I can physically feel the changes going on inside me already," Grassina said joyfully. "And I'm so proud of it!"

"This is such an interesting adventure," Shampina said. "Things are happening nearly to all of us, making us change for the better."

"This forest is enchanted, probably that's why it's like that," Willay said. "Whatever it is, I am glad that I've changed. Now I wish I could find Fountain and apologize."

Chapter 5. Fountain

"The mosquitoes are coming back again!" Rainbow screamed, interrupting the conversation and brandishing her sunshine flashlight over her head. The mosquitoes couldn't come close to her because of the flashlight, so they left, but at that moment unfortunately the flashlight got tangled among the branches and snapped into half. It turned off immediately.

"Oh, no!" Rainbow called. She was in complete darkness, and Shampina, who was also carrying Blowie, fell upon her, as she hadn't noticed that there was someone there.

"Ouch!" Rainbow called. "Get off me, girls!"

"Sorry, I didn't see you were there," Shampina exclaimed.

"What's happened, Rainbow?" Blowie asked. "Why did you break you flashlight?"

"I didn't do it on purpose!" Rainbow said. "It just got tangled among the branches."

"Don't worry, Rainbow," Raya said. "I will make a new one for you."

"Really?" Rainbow said joyfully. "But it is difficult now for you, isn't it? You're flying."

"It doesn't matter," Raya said. She stopped flying, sat down onto the green grass and clicked her fingers. All the other fairies came to watch what she was doing. She made a sunray flashlight again, which was as bright as the previous one, and gave it to Rainbow.

"It was very nice of you, Raya," Rainbow said. "Camellia, now I can see what you mean by saying really good friends. Raya didn't blame me for breaking the sunshine flashlight, and made a new one instead. I feel so bad for not being nice to Fountain."

Camellia was smiling brighter by each minute. She was glad that her friends were at last seeing that it was important to be nice to others – didn't matter if it's your friend or just someone. She knew it would probably take them a long time till they found Fountain, but she didn't consider the time passed in vain: her friends were becoming nicer fairies, and by becoming nicer, they were also becoming beautiful and kind. And that was all that was needed for being a fairy.

Raya and Fluffy were leading the group, flying in the front. Then came Camellia, and then the others followed.

"Raya, what's that?" Fluffy asked, flying forward. She was pointing in front of her, where there didn't seem to be anything extraordinary.

"What?" Raya asked.

"Seems like mist," Fluffy said. "Fog or something like that."

Raya shrugged, as they flew swiftly. Then something strange happened. Both of them flew right into the fog, except that it wasn't fog, but a soft and warm clingy wall, which was very huge. It wasn't a wall, really, because it was very soft.

"Ouch!" Fluffy screamed from surprise. She looked around and saw that Raya was also on the wall next to her. They couldn't move.

Camellia didn't go forward, seeing that her friends had got stuck onto the transparent and soft wall. The others also stopped, looking at the wall with interest.

"I can't move! I can't get free!" Raya began screaming. "What is this? What is happening?"

Fluffy was also trying to free her wings and fly away, but it was impossible, as the soft wall was sticky and kept them on it.

"Fairies? Are you here?" A voice came from the middle of the wall.

Camellia and the other fairies cast their sunshine flashlights to see where the voice was coming from, and gasped: Fountain was in the middle of the wall, and she seemed to be stuck as well.

"Fountain!" The fairies screamed. "What is this? And what are you doing on this wall?"

"This is not a wall," Fountain said. "This is a spider's web. A giant one."

For a moment no one spoke. The fairies realized the danger that they were in.

"I was crying and flying when I got onto this web," Fountain continued talking. "I couldn't see where I was going because it was a bit dark and I had tears in my eyes. But then I realized what it was."

"And… where… where is the spider now?" Raya asked, trying not to move the web anymore.

"I don't know," Fountain said. "Probably it will return soon from wherever it has gone."

"Oh, and then probably it will eat us!" Fluffy said, shivering from fright.

"Please calm down and don't move," Camellia said. "If you move and shake, you will stick deeper into the web and will have no chance to come out again."

The fairies stayed still.

The fairies stood on a tree branch that was closest to the web, but the made sure not to touch the web.

"We must rescue you until the spider comes back," Willay said.

"But how?" Grassina asked.

No one had the answer.

"I think I know what to do," Blowie said. "I'll create strong wind and will direct it towards the web. It may tear part of the web away."

"Right," Camellia said. "And then, on the count of three, all of us will make fairy dust, meant to dissolve the remaining web, all right?"

"A great idea!" Willay exclaimed. "Only the three of you need to be careful not to fall down or to be thrown away by the wind."

"How can we be careful?" Fluffy asked. "We can't even move. I'm sure the wind will blow us away together with the web. I can't move my hands and feet, and when I try to fly, the web pulls me back."

"When the web gets torn away, then the pieces of the web will be easy to throw away, don't worry," Rainbow said. "All right, Blowie, do your magic!"

Blowie clicked her fingers, which created very strong wind – just like the one that she had created when they were still looking for Fountain.

Immediately there came a loud whistle of the wind, threatening to turn everything upside down.

"Girls, hold onto the branches!" Blowie screamed to the fairies that were standing on the branch. The wind blew right onto the thick spider web, momentarily tearing it in half. Camellia and the other fairies held onto the branch as tightly as they could, as they felt the strong wave of the wind swooshing past them instantly.

Shrieking, Fountain, Fluffy and Raya were thrown away on pieces of web they were on. Luckily, Raya was able to use her wings and to fly a bit to the side, away from the wind. Her hands and feet were still stuck onto the web. She looked around and saw that Fluffy and Fountain were also kind of safe – floating downwards towards the ground, still stuck on pieces of web. The wind stopped blowing as fast as it had started.

"On the count of three, fairies! One, two, three!" Camellia screamed, and a thick layer of sparkling fairy dust was emitted into the night air. The sparkles flew everywhere and covered the webs that the three fairies were on. The fairy dust particles managed to dissolve the thick web, making it disappear, and soon Fountain, Fluffy and Raya were flying towards the branch their friends were on.

Chapter 6. The Importance of Being Nice

For a moment no one spoke. The fairies were looking at one another, not sure if they could start a conversation. Then Camellia said:

"Fountain, please forgive all of us..."

"Camellia, you are wrong!" Willay interrupted. "You are the kindest, the nicest and the most pleasant fairy in the forest. It's us who must apologize."

"Yes, and we do it with honesty," Shampina added.

"Please forgive us for hurting you," Blowie said. "We had tried to make a joke, but it turned out that we were actually making fun of you, without even realizing it, but it was so wrong."

"We were not nice to you, and now we have realized that we were wrong," Rainbow said. "I am sure we will never behave that way."

"On our way we came across many challenges, which made us think twice," Raya said. "And from now on all of us have decided to think before speaking, and to make only such jokes that we'd like to be made on us. Jokes can also hurt people's feelings."

"And you know what?" Fluffy said. "By sticking onto this web with you, I saw that all of us were equal, as the three of us were in the same danger and needed to be rescued by the others. We needed help as much as you did, Fountain."

"No one must stand out, as everyone is equal to the others," Raya said. "And you, Fountain, are no exception. We all are equal to you. And we are glad to have you as a friend."

"Fountain," Grassina said. "The dance party was so boring and lonesome without you. I am sure we would not have much fun without you. We want to get you back. We missed you."

Fountain started to smile. "Dear fairies, of course I forgive you! You have come a long way after me, only to say you're sorry for making fun of me. It's really nice of you, and now I feel that I have real friends. You also forgive me for being sensitive, but from now on I may recognize the joke from the teasing and hopefully there will not be such misunderstandings anymore."

All the fairies were happy, but the happiest of them was Camellia, as her dream of making everyone nice had come true, and the fairies of the forest were nice and kind to the others.

***

When the nine fairies returned back to the dancing area, it was already early morning. Though the sun hadn't come out yet, but it was a bit light and cool. There was no one at the dancing area. The fairies approached the party area and stopped there.

"Our party decorations are still here, though the other fairies and the birds are gone," Camellia said. "Probably they have gone to sleep."

"We can take some rest and continue our dance party," Grassina said. "And I am more than sure that it will be the best dance party ever!"

"I think we can also make the decorations more beautiful," Willay added. "After all, we all have changed for the better, so the decorations can also be changed for the better. For example, I think we can add some colorful balloons and shining stars in the air, as well."

"Yes, and the clouds must not only be for sitting down," Fluffy said. "I can create more clouds for floating in the air."

"Wonderful idea!" Fountain said. "And I'll add more fountains on the edges of the dancing area."

"Excellent!" Shampina said, happily jumping up and down. "Fountain, will you dance with us when the party begins?"

"Of course!" Fountain said, giggling. "And I will make sure that my hair sticks out in all the directions."

The fairies started laughing, together with her. Camellia looked at them, smiled and nodded. Everything was well.

- End -

Made in the USA
Middletown, DE
06 January 2018